W9-BSL-547

About the Book

When Roger first looked up at the tree house, he thought he saw something moving at the window. No one should be there—the tree house belonged to the Mayfairs. It was in the deep woods that surrounded their new house in the country.

Still, strange things happened each time Roger and his sister, Anabelle, tried to explore the tree house. Once Roger heard mysterious noises. Another time they found odd-shaped footprints. . . .

What *was* the secret the tree house was hiding?

Weekly Reader Books presents

The
Tree House
Mystery

The Tree House Mystery

By CAROL BEACH YORK

Illustrated by
Reisie Lonette

COWARD, McCANN & GEOGHEGAN, INC.
NEW YORK

This book is a presentation of
Weekly Reader Books.
Weekly Reader Books offers
book clubs for children from
preschool to young adulthood. All
quality hardcover books are selected
by a distinguished Weekly Reader
Selection Board.

For further information write to:
Weekly Reader Books
1250 Fairwood Ave.
Columbus, Ohio 43216

Text copyright © 1973 by Carol Beach York
Illustrations copyright © 1973 by Reisie Lonette

All rights reserved. This book, or parts thereof, may not
be reproduced in any form without permission in writing
from the publishers. Published simultaneously in Canada
by Longman Canada Limited, Toronto.

SBN: GB-698-30488-8
SBN: TR-698-20236-8

Library of Congress Catalog Card Number: 72-85621
Printed in the United States of America

To my friend, Janet Brodesky,
because she likes my stories

The Tree House Mystery

One

When Roger's mother and father decided to buy a house in the country, Roger was not sure whether he was glad or not.

Moving from town meant giving up a lot, he thought. The carnival that came to the vacant lot near his house every summer. Riding his bike around the neighborhood after school. It meant leaving his best friend Bobby Thompson. . . . Roger thought about all this as he sat in the back seat of the car poking slowly along the road from the country house to the woods beyond.

"I'll give you a drive around the property," the real estate man had said. Roger's father sat in the front seat of the car with the real estate man, and Roger's mother sat in the back seat with Roger on one side of her and his sister, Anabelle, on the other. Anabelle had the window rolled down and her head hanging out with strands of yellow hair blowing against her cheeks.

"The children are going to love this place," the

real estate man said, glancing in his rearview mirror.

"Oh, I know they will," Mrs. Mayfair answered with a smile.

I won't, Roger thought. I like living in town.

Behind them the house where they were going to be living was cut off from sight as the real estate man turned onto the path that led through the woods. He was perspiring in the July heat, but his broad red-cheeked face was beaming.

"You've got a great buy here, Mr. Mayfair," he said to Roger's father. "That's a good, comfortable house, and you've got this beautiful woods. There's even a little creek." He smiled into the rearview mirror again. "Just right for wading."

"Do you hear that, children?" Mrs. Mayfair said.

Anabelle hung her head farther out the window, squinting up into the sunlight that filtered down between the trees. She was seven and as usual had a doll beside her on the car seat and a ribbon working its way loose from her ponytail. "Anabelle just isn't a neat little girl," Roger's mother often said to her friends. Now Mrs. Mayfair was picturing Anabelle in days to come, wading in a creek and playing in a woods. Mrs. Mayfair could see lots of muddy shoes and torn dresses, but she didn't mind because she was so happy about buying the house in the country.

"How about that, Roger?" she said. "A creek."

"Yeah, that's swell. . . ."

Was a creek as good as a carnival in the vacant lot?

What about the secret notes he and Bobby Thompson left for each other under the flower pot by Bobby's garage?

Could you ride a bike through the woods? Roger looked doubtfully at the bumpy dirt road.

"There's a rabbit!" Anabelle cried, stretching a thin tan little arm out of the car window. Roger looked just in time to see a blob of brown fur disappearing into the brush beside the road.

"You'll see lots of things here, little lady," the real estate man said with a broad grin. "Squirrels, rabbits, chipmunks."

"It's so beautiful here in the woods." Mrs. Mayfair sighed contentedly. Roger's father smiled back at her from the front seat. They had been saving to buy land in the country since they were first married. It was a dream come true for them to have twenty-three acres, a big white frame farm house, and a woods of their own.

Roger began to notice that the woods were thick now. Not much sunlight came through the trees.

"Here's something the children will really like," the real estate man said. He slowed the car to a stop beside a small clearing in the woods and pointed to a large tree. "There's a tree house up in that tree. The kids will have a lot of fun there."

"A tree house!" Roger's mother echoed with delight. "Isn't that marvelous!"

Everyone looked out the car windows, up into the branches of the tree. They could see the platform of boards and a wall with an opening like a tiny window. But they couldn't see too much because of the leaves.

There was a ladder of boards nailed into the tree trunk.

"Let's go up," Anabelle begged, but Mr. Mayfair said, "I'm afraid we can't today, honey. We've got so many other things to do. You'll have lots of days to play here after we move."

Roger looked up at the tree house. It looked

mysterious, he thought, way up there, half-hidden by the tree branches. And then just as the real estate man started to drive on, Roger thought he saw something move in the little window of the tree house. He looked back through the rear window of the car, but soon the tree house was out of sight. He couldn't be sure what he had seen—or if he really had seen anything.

"Hey," he started to say, "I saw—"

But just then the real estate man said something to Roger's father, and nobody heard Roger.

"The woods are really deep here," Mrs. Mayfair remarked.

And sort of spooky, Roger thought. He was glad when the car made a turn and came out on the highway.

"We've covered all the length of your new property, Mr. Mayfair," the real estate man said. The car picked up speed once they were out of the woods.

"We didn't see the creek," Anabelle protested.

"That's just a ways past the tree house, but it's in the woods, can't drive a car there," the real estate man explained. "You and your brother will have to find that on foot."

"I wanted to go wading today," Anabelle said.

"There will be lots of days for that," her mother told her. She drew Anabelle close to her and put her arm around her and smoothed the tangled yellow hair. Anabelle hugged her doll and watched the countryside flying by.

That night, back in town, Roger wrote a note to Bobby Thompson. It said: "We are moving next week. We have a creek and a tree house."

He left the note under the flower pot by Bobby's garage.

It was probably the last note he would be writing to Bobby.

And there wouldn't be many more nights to sleep in his old room. The houses along the street were lighted in the dusk. And the ice-cream truck went by with its bell ringing. It was a lot different from the quiet woods they had driven through that afternoon.

Roger got into bed and lay awhile looking up at his ceiling.

Had he really seen something move in the tree house window?

Two

After that, the days flew by with a bustle of packing and moving. Roger did not have much time to think about the tree house, and he began to forget how dark and spooky it had been in the woods. Maybe living in the country was going to be fun after all. He and Anabelle would ride a bus to school when summer was over.

"How will you get to school?" Bobby Thompson had wanted to know.

"We ride a bus bus bus," Anabelle chanted.

Bobby looked envious.

"And we've got a creek to wade in."

"You can come and visit us when we're settled, Bobby," Roger's mother said. Bobby had played with Roger so long Mrs. Mayfair felt as if he were part of her family. She would miss his plump little face popping up almost daily at her kitchen door.

There were lots of trips made back and forth to the house in the country. Boxes of books and dishes and clothes seemed to be everywhere, in everyone's way, whether it was the house in town or the house in the country.

The Mayfairs were going to sell the house in town, but at least temporarily they had two houses. "It's nice not to have to move all in one day," Mrs. Mayfair told her neighbor lady friends.

Anabelle flitted around with her dolls and falling hair bows, and Roger and Bobby sat on up-ended packing boxes and kicked their rubber-soled canvas shoes against the sides and licked popsicles. Summer was getting a good start now, and they were glad school was over.

23

"You'll miss the carnival," Bobby reminded Roger.

"Oh, I don't know about that." Mr. Mayfair was passing by with an armload of tools to put in the car. "We'll get into town now and then. We aren't moving to the end of the world, you know."

Roger felt better and better all the time about moving to the country. They weren't going to miss the carnival, after all; that was something.

But sometimes before he fell asleep at night, Roger would look sadly around his room. It was bare now of all the things he had tacked on the walls. Some of his things were already out in the house in the country. By the dark woods.

One day, when they had driven out with a carload of things from the house in town, Roger and Anabelle went exploring in the woods.

"You two go and see if you can find that creek the real estate agent told us about," Mr. Mayfair suggested.

24

"If we find it, can we wade?" Anabelle asked eagerly.

Mrs. Mayfair smiled. "Yes, go ahead and wade if you want to," she said. "I guess I'd better start getting used to you two having a whole woods to play in."

"Can we go up in the tree house?"

But at that, Mrs. Mayfair shook her head.

"Not today, Anabelle. Sometime Daddy will go with you and check to be sure there aren't any rotting boards in the floor or weak places in that tree ladder."

"But we'll be careful," Anabelle begged.

"Not today," Mr. Mayfair said firmly. "I'll go check the tree house one of these days soon. Right now I've got *this* house on my mind."

"Oh, phooey." Anabelle had the last word and trudged off with Roger, a doll under each arm.

"Don't go too far away," Mrs. Mayfair called after them.

They walked along, away from the house and

yard and into the woods. The dirt road was streaked with sunlight at first, where the woods were thin. But as they walked farther, the path began to get darker. Now and then a bird rustled the leaves in the branches above their heads, and Anabelle darted from one side to another picking wild flowers.

"I want to find a rabbit," she said to Roger. "If I find it, maybe we can keep it for a pet."

"Maybe," Roger agreed.

"Do you think Mama will let us?"

Roger didn't know. But before he could answer, Anabelle ran away along the path. Roger could

see her ahead . . . and then nearby, somewhere in the trees, Roger heard twigs cracking, as if someone were walking close to him but hidden by the trees. Roger stopped. The sound of cracking twigs stopped, too. Everything was quiet in the woods. Roger looked hard into the woods. But there were only the trees . . . and then Anabelle was calling back to him, "Hurry up, Roger—here's the tree house—"

Ahead Roger could see the cleared place beside the road, and the great thick-branched old tree, and the tree house. Anabelle was leaning against the trunk, trying to wiggle the boards that had been nailed up for a ladder.

"I want to go up," she insisted. But she stayed on the ground. "I wonder if there's anything inside," she said. "Do you think they have furniture in tree houses?"

"I don't know."

Roger came to the foot of the tree and peered up through the branches. He could see the bottom of the platform floor, but not much else. Whatever was above the ladder would be unknown until they could climb up and look for themselves.

Roger squinted his eyes to see better, but he couldn't see anything moving at the window, as he had the time before.

Anabelle sat down in the grass beside the tree and spread her wild flowers in her lap.

Beyond in the woods a twig cracked, and then another, as if someone were walking in the woods. It was just like the sounds Roger had heard on the path. He looked over his shoulder, into the deep shadowy woods.

"Hey, Anabelle, did you hear something?"

Anabelle looked up at him, pushing strands of hair from her eyes.

She had been too busy with her flowers.

"I thought I heard something," Roger whispered. "Like somebody walking. Listen."

They were both very quiet. But there were no more sounds of footsteps from the woods.

"Who's here, who's here, who's here?" Anabelle chanted.

But there was no answer.

"There's no one here," she said with a shrug.

But Roger was not so sure.

Three

Anabelle liked the creek and the woods and all the flowers she found growing in secret places.

But mostly she wanted to climb up into that tree house.

"All right, Miss Pesty," Mr. Mayfair said one day soon after they had moved into the country house, "today we'll go and see if the tree house is safe."

Anabelle began to clap her hands. "We're going to the tree house tree house tree house."

It would be more fun if Bobby Thompson were here, Roger thought. But he was excited about

31

climbing up into the tree house at last. He wondered what it would be like up there high in the tree branches.

"Come on then, kids." Mr. Mayfair was ready to go. "I'm interested in seeing what that tree house is like myself."

"And I'm going to get this kitchen in order," Mrs. Mayfair said. She was thinking how nice it would be to have some uninterrupted time to putter around her nice big house in the country. In a few more days she would have shelf paper in the kitchen cabinets, curtains at the windows, and flowers in the flower boxes. She set about her work, humming happily to herself, as Mr. Mayfair and Anabelle and Roger started off through the woods.

Mr. Mayfair tested the tree ladder carefully. Each board seemed securely and safely in place, and he went up while Anabelle and Roger waited curiously below.

At the top of the ladder, Mr. Mayfair disappeared from sight in the tree branches, and Roger could hear him stamping on the floor boards of the tree house. After a few moments his head appeared, and he called down to them: "OK, kids. But come up carefully."

"Me first!" Anabelle shouted. She pushed her dolls at Roger to hold and grasped the ladder with both hands. The boards stuck out from the sides of the tree and made good handholds, and in a moment Anabelle too was up in the tree house.

"Throw up my dolls," she called back to Roger. She was lying on her stomach on the tree house floor, waving her arms down through the tree branches.

Roger tossed up a limp rag doll with no shoes, and it fell back down as Anabelle stretched her hands but missed it.

"Roger's throwing up my dolls, but I can't catch them," Anabelle cried.

Mr. Mayfair knelt beside Anabelle, and Roger

34

tried again. This time Mr. Mayfair caught the flying bundle of cotton skirts and yarn hair.

The second doll was a rubber baby doll with a blue bonnet and booties. Roger aimed carefully and tossed it up, and his father caught it easily.

"Now I'm coming up," Roger called. He felt as if he were giving a warning—but he wasn't sure exactly why. Surely nothing strange could be up in the tree house. His father and Anabelle would have seen it. . . .

Grasping the outer ends of the boards, Roger began to climb up into the tree house.

Four

"Look, Roger, there's a table table table," Anabelle was chanting.

In the middle of the tree house floor was a small three-legged stool, and Anabelle had already seated herself on the floor beside it with her dolls. It was just the right size for a table for them.

Mr. Mayfair had to stoop inside the tree house, but it was big enough for Roger to stand up straight. He could touch the roof with his hands. There were two walled sides, each with a small square opening like a window. The other two sides had railings.

36

Except for the stool, Anabelle's "table," the little room was bare. And yet Roger had a funny feeling, as if something or someone were watching him from somewhere . . . or a hand might suddenly touch his shoulder . . . or a voice whisper in his ear.

"You aren't listening, Roger," his father was saying. "I said, you two mustn't hang over these side railings when you play up here. And you must always be careful going up and down the ladder."

"We will," Roger promised. He was standing by one of the windows—the window where he had thought he saw something move. It was just the height of his head, and he could see down to the clearing through an open space in the tree branches. He could see the road where the real estate man had driven his car away from the clearing.

On the opposite wall, the window looked out to the woods beyond. Mr. Mayfair bent down and peered out of that window, and Anabelle whispered to her dolls.

"This will be a nice place for you to play," Mr. Mayfair said. He was a little uncomfortable, bending down so much. But he could see that the tree house boards were sound and safe.

Roger went to the back of the tree house, where a railing had been nailed up from wall to wall. The railing was about as high as his shoulders. He stood looking down into the woods. And listening. Everything was quiet. But why did he have the feeling that someone was there, watching them? Someone or something knew they were in the tree house, someone or something out there somewhere in the woods.

"Look what I found," Anabelle called out suddenly. She was holding up a small piece of bread.

Mr. Mayfair hunched around and tried to get in a more comfortable position.

"It was right here under the table," Anabelle said. "Daddy, where would a piece of bread come from?"

"Well, don't eat it," Mr. Mayfair warned. "Some bird probably dropped it out of his beak. You know how your mother throws out stale bread to the birds. Here, let's throw it back down into the clearing. It will make a good supper for some sparrow."

"But this is nice and soft," Anabelle said.

"Well, anyway, let's just throw it back into the clearing."

Roger and Anabelle watched as Mr. Mayfair dropped the scrap of bread through the railing to the ground below. No bird came swooping to claim it as his lost supper. Everything was quiet around the tree house. Not even a small breeze stirred the leaves today.

It was *too* quiet, Roger thought. There ought to be birds chirping in the trees and squirrels running along the branches. Maybe it was a bird perched on the window he had seen before—or a squirrel.

"You two want to stay here and play awhile?" Mr. Mayfair had done about all the stooping over he could take for the time.

"My dolls are having lunch," Anabelle explained. She had knelt down again by the three-legged stool and was staring at the rag doll and the blue-bonneted baby doll. "Eat your vegetables," she said to them.

Mr. Mayfair went down the ladder and waved back to Roger and Anabelle. "If you go wading in the creek, try not to get your clothes too wet," he called up to them.

Roger sat down on the floor by Anabelle. There didn't seem much for him to do in the tree house. When Anabelle had her dolls, she was always busy with them. If he was home now, home in *town,* he'd be riding his bike with Bobby Thompson and some of the other guys along the block. Maybe they'd have dimes for ice cream, and they'd ride around looking for the ice-cream man. He bet that was just what Bobby and the other guys were doing right now. The tree house wasn't as much fun as that.

"This table has a crooked leg," Anabelle was fussing. "It wiggles."

She rocked the stool back and forth.

But Roger wasn't listening. He was looking at a piece of yellow paper wedged between the floorboards in the corner of the tree house. He hadn't noticed it before. It made him think about

the secret notes he and Bobby Thompson wrote. The tree house would be a good place to leave secret notes, if only Bobby Thompson didn't live so far away in town.

Roger tugged at the corner of the paper, and it came up from the boards, folded and wrinkly. And there was writing on it . . . he *had* found a secret note.

His heart began to beat faster as he read the unexpected message.

Five

"I am not coming here anymore. I am afraid
The Thing will come back. You better not
come here anymore, too. It is too dangerous.
Meet me by the old tree. *But don't come back
up here.*"

Roger stared at the words. He felt prickles
along his arms.

I am afraid The Thing will come back.

A sound startled him and he jerked around—
not knowing what to expect! But it was only
Anabelle moving her stool-table.

43

"Anabelle, look what I found—"

Roger held out the wrinkled scrap of paper.

"What is it?" Anabelle looked up at the paper curiously.

"It's a note, a secret note. It was stuck between the boards."

"Who would write us a note?"

"It's not for us. Somebody left it up here for somebody else."

"What does it say?"

"It says, 'I'm not coming here anymore. I am afraid The Thing—'" Roger hesitated. He didn't want to scare Anabelle. But it was too late now.

"What thing?" Anabelle wanted to know.

Roger read the rest of the note aloud. "I am afraid The Thing will come back. You better not come here anymore, too. It is too dangerous. Meet me by the old tree. But don't come back up here."

Anabelle stared up with wide eyes. "What thing?" she asked again. "What thing is coming back?"

But Roger had already started for the tree house ladder.

"Come on," he called. "I'm going to show this to Daddy."

Anabelle scrambled up and hurried after Roger, and they ran all the way home along the path through the woods.

Mrs. Mayfair was at the kitchen sink when Roger and Anabelle burst through the door. Mr.

Mayfair was sitting at the table drinking a cup of coffee. He looked up with surprise.

"What, home so soon?" Mr. Mayfair started to ask, but Roger was already pulling the secret note out of his pocket.

"Look what we found in the tree house!"

"I thought you were going wading." Mrs. Mayfair turned from the sink. She could see the children had been running hard. Anabelle was gasping for breath.

Mr. Mayfair drew the note across the table and read it. Mrs. Mayfair came and stood by his chair and leaned forward to read the note too.

"Roger found it in the boards," Anabelle panted.

"What boards?" Mrs. Mayfair looked up, frowning.

"I found it stuck in the corner of the tree house. I thought it might be a note, like Bobby and I write—and it was—"

46

"What's The Thing, Mama?" Anabelle tugged at her mother's arm. "Is it coming back?"

But Mr. Mayfair began to smile. "It's a secret note all right. But you know where I think it came from. Probably the children who lived here before and played in the tree house left it there. I bet it was some game they were playing, and it's been stuck up in that tree house since they left."

"Do you think so?" Roger looked at the paper again. It did look kind of old and wrinkled-up. Maybe it had been there a long time.

"Yes, I'm sure that's the answer," his mother said reassuringly. "The children were just playing a game of some kind, and this note was part of it. 'Meet me at the old tree.' That's probably part of the game."

"But what's The Thing?" Anabelle persisted, her small face upturned to her mother.

"Just part of the game, I expect," Mrs. Mayfair said.

47

"Oh." Anabelle twisted a strand of hair.

"I'm sure the children who lived here before had lots of fun leaving notes around in places in the woods," Mrs. Mayfair added. "Maybe if you find 'the old tree,' you'll find some more notes there."

"How can we find an old tree?" Roger protested. He waved his arms helplessly. There were so *many* trees.

Mr. Mayfair laughed. "It could keep you busy all summer," he agreed. "Look for a tree with a hole in the trunk. That would be a good hiding place for notes."

"Let's go look now," Anabelle said to Roger. She was not frightened anymore. If she had not yet found a rabbit, she might find notes in trees.

Roger folded up the note and put it in his pocket again. He followed Anabelle down the back porch steps. But he couldn't help thinking how he had seen something at the tree house window once and how he had heard twigs crunching in the woods as if somebody were walking there. Maybe it had been The Thing.

Maybe the note wasn't just a game some other children had been playing long ago.

Maybe it was a real warning.

Six

Roger and Anabelle looked all the rest of the afternoon. But they didn't find any notes in hollow trees.

Roger listened all the time, but he didn't hear any strange noises, as if The Thing were walking in the woods.

"I guess those other children took all their notes." Anabelle gave up at last.

They walked home together, and Roger began to feel better. Lots of things could make noises in the woods—squirrels and rabbits. The real estate man had said they would find lots of them in the woods. And chipmunks, too. That was probably all he had heard before. There wasn't really anything to be afraid of in the woods or at the tree house.

The next day Mrs. Mayfair said Roger and Anabelle could take a picnic lunch to the tree house.

Roger stood at the kitchen table and spread peanut butter in thick globs on slices of bread. That was his favorite kind of sandwich, and when he made it himself, he put on about twice as much peanut butter as his mother used.

Anabelle had to have jelly on her peanut butter sandwiches, and she stood at Roger's elbow, chanting, "Don't forget my jelly jelly jelly."

"Roger, you don't need a whole jar of peanut butter for one sandwich," his mother scolded. But she was smiling.

Outside, a warm sun shone brightly, and along the roadway a few cars went by flashing in the sunlight. There was another house a short distance down the road, but beyond that the countryside stretched as far as you could see.

"Today I start getting the closets in order," Mrs. Mayfair announced. She loved putting things in their right places, and she loved having all the room of this big house in the country. She opened a package of store cookies, and because she was happy about her new house and the warm sunny day, she put an extra big number of cookies into a paper bag for Roger and Anabelle. When she was settled, she would bake cookies. Pies would cool on the windowsills of the big kitchen. Maybe she would bake bread some days. It seemed the right thing to do in a house in the country.

"Can we have apples?" Anabelle begged. She came out of the pantry with an apple in each hand.

"Yes, you can take apples if you like," Mrs. Mayfair said. "Wash them first."

"We can wash them in the creek," Roger said. He licked the peanut butter knife and put it in the sink with the unwashed breakfast dishes.

"When are you coming to our tree house, Mama?" Anabelle put the apples in the lunch bag and squashed the top closed.

"I'll come one day soon," Mrs. Mayfair promised.

"I let my dollies sleep in the tree house all night," Anabelle chattered. "Can *I* do that sometime, Mama?"

Mrs. Mayfair hesitated. "I don't know, honey."

"Please please please."

Mrs. Mayfair laughed. "Go on now, I have a lot to do today."

They went to the creek first and washed their apples. Anabelle lay on her stomach by the water and looked at her reflection. The tips of her hair hung down past her face and dangled in the water.

Roger took off his shoes and waded across the creek. It was stony on the bottom, but not too bad once you got used to it.

He scooped up a handful of the pebbles and admired them in the sunlight. Some were greenish-pink; some were gray. Maybe he would start a collection, he thought. At home—he still thought of the house in town as "home"—he had had a collection of leaves one summer, and another time he had a collection of bottle caps. Bobby Thompson had bottle caps, too, and they tried to see who could get the most. Every time anyone at Roger's house opened a bottle of soda Roger got the cap. And sometimes he found caps on the street, but not too often. Bobby Thompson used to find caps in the vacant lot, but Roger had never found any there, although he had looked lots of times. Bobby Thompson had the most bottle caps when school started. Then he had brought them all to Roger one day.

"My mom says I have too much junk in my

room, so you can have my bottle caps," he said to Roger.

"This is my lucky day," Mrs. Mayfair had remarked. Like Bobby's mother, Mrs. Mayfair thought Roger already had more than he needed crammed into the drawers and places of his little bedroom.

But now, in this country house, Roger had a much bigger room. He had room for lots of collections. Maybe he would collect pebbles in the creek and give some to Bobby Thompson when he came to visit.

Roger waded all the way across the creek—and then he saw something that made him forget about Bobby Thompson and collecting pebbles.

The ground at the edge of the creek was muddy, and there, clearly outlined in the damp earth, were a lot of large, strange-looking footprints. They were long and narrow, nearly as long as Roger's arm, and there were three toes at one end.

Roger gazed down at the prints in astonishment.

"Did you find another note?" Anabelle came splashing after him.

"Look at *these*." Roger pointed to the ground. "What kind of animal made *these*?"

"A rabbit?" Anabelle looked at the ground and then up at Roger hopefully.

"A *rabbit*—heck, no. Rabbits have little paws."

"Maybe a big rabbit?"

Maybe The Thing, Roger was thinking. But he didn't want to scare Anabelle.

"Maybe The Thing?" Anabelle was remembering the note, too.

She looked worried, and Roger said quickly, "That was just a game, Anabelle. Those kids just made that up when they wrote that note."

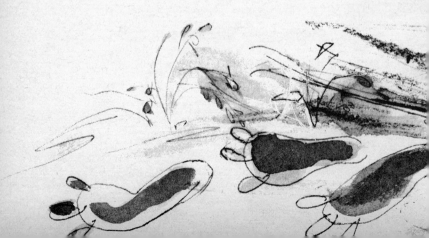

They stood looking at the prints uneasily, and at last Roger said, "Come on, it's time to eat lunch."

They waded back across the creek and put on their shoes again, pushing hard to get their wet feet inside. Then they walked to the tree house, with their cookies and sandwiches. And the apples they had washed in the creek.

They had barely reached the clearing when Anabelle let out a shout.

"My dolly has fallen out of the tree!"

She ran ahead of Roger across the long grass, her feet squishing in her shoes. There at the foot of the tree ladder lay the rag doll in a crumpled heap, a bright red blob in the grass. She had landed on her head.

"Oh, my poor dolly," Anabelle crooned, taking the doll in her arms. "How did you fall down?"

Through a tangle of yarn hair the rag doll stared back from two glass eyes.

Roger stood swinging the bag with the lunch.

How could the doll have gotten up from the stool-table where Anabelle had left her and fallen down out of the tree?

But there she was.

Roger looked up doubtfully. In the branches above his head the tree house loomed silently. Not a board creaked; not a sound could be heard.

Seven

"I have to go see my other doll," Anabelle was saying as she started to scramble up the ladder with the rag doll in one hand.

"Be careful," Roger called. He put the top of the lunch bag between his teeth and climbed up after her. He had wanted to say, "Wait, Anabelle, maybe something's up there!" But she had gone so fast.

However, there was nothing unusual in the tree house. And the baby doll with her blue bonnet still sat on the floor by the three-legged stool. Roger was not sure what he had expected to find

. . . something that made long footprints by the creek, perhaps.

"You're a good baby," Anabelle said to the doll by the stool. "Naughty Raggy Annie fell out."

"She couldn't fall out all by herself," Roger argued.

"Sure she could," Anabelle said. "She walked right over and tried to climb down the ladder, and she fell."

"Dolls can't walk."

"They can walk when nobody's looking," Anabelle insisted. "At least Raggy Annie can. Baby Blue hasn't learned yet."

Roger sat down by the stool and opened the paper bag. He got out his big fat peanut butter sandwich.

Anabelle broke a cookie in two and put a piece in front of each doll.

"Dolls can't eat," Roger said. His words didn't come out very well, he had so much gluey peanut butter in his mouth.

"They can so eat." Anabelle dripped jelly on her blouse and tried to scoop it up with her finger. "Dolls can eat and walk and talk and everything. They just don't do it when people are around."

"Who told you that?"

"Mary Jo."

Mary Jo was a little girl who had come to play with Anabelle when they lived in town. She was tall and skinny, and she was about two years older than Anabelle; but Mrs. Mayfair had said she was glad to have Mary Jo come any time, because there were so few little girls for Anabelle to play with.

Roger chewed his sandwich and thought about skinny Mary Jo. When Anabelle wasn't looking, he ate the rag doll's piece of cookie.

"See," Anabelle exclaimed when she noticed the cookie was gone. "Raggy Annie ate her cookie already. Now she can have another."

Roger couldn't stop thinking about those footprints by the creek. Maybe dolls *could* walk and

Raggy Annie had tried to escape. Escape what? Roger's thoughts wandered uncertainly. Outside, the day which had started so brightly was beginning to darken. Thunder rumbled in the distance.

"Time for your naps," Anabelle said to her dolls. She yanked them up from the floor and went over to a corner. "This is your bedroom," she said to them. "I'm going down and get some leaves to make you a nice soft bed."

Roger finished his sandwich and rolled up the waxed paper. It was quiet in the tree house, now that Anabelle had gone down the ladder to find some leaves.

Roger ate his apple and looked out at the darkening sky. They would have to go home soon. A storm was coming. But first there was something he wanted to find out. He wanted to find out if whatever made those footprints had been around the tree house.

Anabelle came up the ladder with leaves in her pockets. If there were any footprints around the tree house, she had been too busy gathering leaves to notice.

The prints were not so clear in the dry ground by the tree house. But they were there, two prints close by the tree. Long and narrow with three toes.

It was The Thing, Roger was sure! It had been at the creek, and it had been around the tree house. Maybe even up into it!

A few drops of rain began to fall, and the thunder rumbled again.

"It's raining—"Anabelle came down the ladder. She didn't like thunder.

Roger turned away from the prints quickly. He didn't want Anabelle to see them and be afraid.

"We better get home," he said. "Let's run."

Anabelle put her hand in his, and they began to run along the path toward home. A sharp wind had risen and tossed the branches of the trees as they raced along.

Around them, in the wind, they seemed to hear strange sounds. And they ran as though The Thing itself were at their heels!

Eight

"Probably a squirrel got up in the tree house and tried to carry the doll in his mouth," Mrs. Mayfair said. "Or maybe tried to play with it and knocked it off through the railing."

"Raggy Annie was trying to climb down the ladder, and she fell," Anabelle insisted.

Mrs. Mayfair smoothed Anabelle's wet hair. "Maybe so, honey," she said, smiling.

The kitchen windows streamed with rain, and the thunder crashed overhead.

"And we saw footprints by the creek," Anabelle

said. "Big footprints, this long." She held her hands wide apart.

"My goodness, that long?" Mrs. Mayfair pretended to be surprised. She was used to Anabelle exaggerating things.

"They were, Mama," Roger said.

"A big rabbit made them," Anabelle said. "If I find that big rabbit, can I keep it, Mama? Please can I? I can keep it in my bedroom."

Mrs. Mayfair laughed. "If its feet are that big, it must be a pretty big rabbit. It might not fit in your bedroom."

Roger wished it hadn't started to rain. He wanted Daddy to go and look at those footprints and tell him what could make them. But now they would be all washed away by the rain.

And he wanted to say, "Something's been up in our tree house—something followed us through the woods; I heard twigs cracking." But Anabelle hadn't heard anything. "Who's here?" she had called. And no one answered. They would prob-

ably only laugh at him and say his imagination was "running away with him." That's what they were always saying to him. It always made Roger think of a tall, thin man in a black cape, like a magician, seizing Roger by the hand and rushing him away into a sky swirling with clouds. Mr. Imagination runs away with Roger.

That night, when it was dark in the woods beyond his bedroom window, Roger thought about the tree house. He thought about the creek lying in the night with the pebbles glimmering in the moonlight under the cool surface of the water. But mostly he thought about the tree house, and how dark it would be there now, with the branches stirring softly in the wind about the wooden walls.

Was anybody there now, in the tree house in the dark night in the dark woods?

He pulled the covers closer up around his chin and shivered. He seemed to see the tree house as it would be at nighttime with the windows like blank eyes staring out into the blackness. And inside, Anabelle's two little dolls lying on their pile of leaves in the corner.

If dolls really could walk, would Raggy Annie try to run away again? Would something frighten them as they lay there in the middle of the dark woods?

Nine

The next morning after breakfast Anabelle wanted to go get her dolls from the tree house.

"Put on some shoes, Roger, and go along with Anabelle," Mrs. Mayfair said. She thought Anabelle was too little to go off into the woods alone.

Roger was sitting at the kitchen table looking at a magazine that had pictures of astronauts and rockets. He thought he might be an astronaut someday, and he was going to practice up by riding all the highest, fastest rides when the carnival came to town. He didn't want to think anymore about the tree house, and here breakfast was hardly over and he had to go right back to it.

He went upstairs to his bedroom and put on his shoes. He sat on the floor and tied the laces slowly.

"Aren't you ever coming!" Anabelle yelled from the foot of the stairs.

But Roger was busy thinking.

At last he got up and went to the desk by his bed. There was a tablet of different colored pages his mother had bought for him in the dime store in town. He sat down at the desk and took one of his pencils. The top sheet in the tablet was green. He licked the pencil and began to print very carefully on the green page: *Stay out. This is our tree house.*

"Ro-ger," Anabelle called again.

Roger tore off the paper and folded it quickly. He shoved it down into his pocket.

He was going to leave the note in the tree house and see what happened.

"I want to find a rabbit rabbit rabbit." Anabelle ran ahead of Roger along the path through the woods. Her face was puckered with a frown as she peered behind bushes and rocks along the way.

"I'm going to start a collection of pebbles from the creek," Roger said. He felt rather daring with the note in his pocket. And a little frightened, too. He didn't want to think about the tree house.

"I want a collection, too," Anabelle said eagerly. She pushed hair out of her eyes. "What can I collect?"

"Well," Roger answered slowly, "maybe you could collect leaves."

"I want to collect pebbles."

"All right," Roger agreed. "You can collect pebbles, too."

The path was growing darker as they got deeper into the woods. First Anabelle ran ahead; then she lagged behind. Her hair ribbon slipped off and lay among the fallen leaves, but she didn't notice. She wanted to find a rabbit and pet its soft fur and look into its little eyes.

Roger reached the edge of the clearing first— and all his bravery about leaving a warning note in the tree house vanished. There was a movement at the tree house window! Someone—or some-thing —was already there! *"Stay out. This is our tree house."* Roger shrank back behind a clump of bushes, his heart pounding.

"Hey, Anabelle——" He grabbed her arm as she came flitting along, a bunch of weeds and flowers clutched in her hand.

"What's the matter——" she started to say, but Roger put his hand over her mouth.

"Be quiet—there's somebody up in the tree house," he whispered fiercely and pulled her back behind the bushes.

Anabelle's eyes widened with surprise. "Who —" she started again, but her voice faded away. Roger looked so strange. It made Anabelle fright-

ened. She pressed close against him, and they peered through the prickly branches into the clearing. Ahead of them the tree house was silent in the great tree.

There was no sound or any other movement at the window.

Anabelle began to fidget. "I want my dollies," she whined.

"We can't go up there now," Roger whispered back. "There's somebody there."

"Let's get Daddy. Somebody is stealing my dollies."

Roger wanted to run away. He wanted to run away from the dark woods and the tree house and never come back.

But if they left, whatever was in the tree house would go away, and they wouldn't know what it was—or when it might come back again!

Roger gazed miserably through the bushes and tried to decide what to do.

At last he said, "You go and get Daddy, and I'll wait here."

"I want my dollies." Anabelle was about to cry.

"I'll wait here and watch and see if anybody takes them," Roger promised. "You go and get Daddy."

"I don't want to go alone—"

"But if I go, too, somebody might take your dollies, and I wouldn't be here to see them."

Anabelle thought about this doubtfully. She lifted a finger and smudged the tears across her cheeks in wet streaks.

"Now go on," Roger urged. "Just go back along the path and get Daddy."

Anabelle looked fearfully back at the path. It had seemed full of pretty flowers and maybe rabbits, if she could only find one. But now it looked lonely and scary.

"Go *on*." Roger pushed her a little toward the path.

Anabelle took a few steps. She turned and looked back at Roger.

"Go *on*."

Anabelle turned and fled back along the path.

Ten

It seemed as if Anabelle were gone a long time. Roger crouched behind the bushes, not daring to take his eyes off the tree house. It loomed above him, silent and secretive. Birds called back and forth between the trees, but otherwise there was no sound.

Then—there was something at the tree house window again. Roger felt a shiver go down his back. Was it a face? It was hard to see clearly through the branches that partly covered the side of the tree house.

He wished Anabelle would get back with Daddy. He had said he would protect Anabelle's dolls, but what would he really do if something started to come down out of the tree house before Daddy got here?

The sun shifted pale through the tree branches to the grassy clearing, and a white butterfly skimmed near Roger, dipping up and down in the dusky light.

And then at last Roger heard them coming. He looked back along the path, and there they were, Daddy first with Anabelle and Mother trailing behind.

Roger was glad to see them. And he was glad that he hadn't run away. Whatever was in the tree house could not escape now.

"There's something up there, Daddy," Roger began excitedly as Mr. Mayfair reached the bushes where Roger was hiding.

Mrs. Mayfair put her arm across Anabelle's

shoulders and stared up at the tree house nervously.

"Probably just some old tramp who was wandering through the woods," Mr. Mayfair said.

Roger's mother looked unhappy to think they had bought land in the country where strangers wandered in their woods. Her arm tightened around Anabelle's shoulders.

Roger's father went boldly into the clearing. He walked toward the tree house, and when he had reached the foot of the tree, he stopped and looked up the ladder to the platform of boards above.

"Who's there?" he called up loudly.

Roger and Anabelle and Mrs. Mayfair came into the clearing slowly.

"Are you sure you saw someone, Roger?" Mr. Mayfair said.

Roger nodded firmly. "I saw something at the window—like a face."

Mr. Mayfair called up again: "Who's there?"

81

But there was no answer. Even the birds were quiet now. There wasn't a sound in the clearing.

"I'll go up and see," Roger's father said after a moment.

"Oh—be careful—" Mrs. Mayfair cautioned. She sounded worried.

Anabelle shivered and kept close to her mother's side. Wisps of hair straggled across her tearstained cheeks.

Roger watched as his father went up the tree ladder. And he wanted to go up, too, now that Daddy was going up. He hardly heard his mother's anxious voice as he started up. "Roger, wait—"

Roger could see his father standing above him by the railing, and as his own eyes reached the level of the tree house floor, Roger could see past the railing into the house. Two boys about Roger's size were crouched back against the wall. On the floor lay a stubby pencil and a yellow tablet . . . the same kind of yellow paper the secret note had been written on.

Eleven

"It's all right," Mr. Mayfair called down to Mrs. Mayfair and Anabelle.

"Be careful, Mama." Anabelle came up the ladder first, with Mrs. Mayfair close behind. They were surprised to see two boys in the tree house, and Anabelle was glad to see that her dolls were all right, still just where she left them sleeping on their bed of leaves.

"My name is Mr. Mayfair," Roger's father said to the two boys.

The boys glanced uneasily at each other, and

one tried to cover the edge of the tablet with his hand. But it was too late. Everyone had seen it.

"Writing some more notes?" Mr. Mayfair asked. His voice was friendly, but the boys looked at each other nervously again.

"It was just—just a joke," one boy said at last.

"You're the Crandon boys, aren't you?" Roger's father said. "I saw you in the yard when I stopped in to speak to your folks the other day."

The Crandon house was the next one down the road. The only one nearby.

"Your house is so close here," Mr. Mayfair said, "I bet you used to play up here in the tree house before we bought the land."

He seemed to understand just how things were.

The boys looked down at the floor silently. Then the one who seemed to be the oldest said, "It was sort of our clubhouse."

"I see." Mr. Mayfair nodded.

"I suppose you thought you wouldn't be able to play here anymore when the property was

sold," Mrs. Mayfair said kindly. Like Mr. Mayfair, she seemed to know how the boys had felt, having the tree house for their clubhouse and then learning that a new family had bought the property.

"And you wanted to scare Roger and Anabelle away by writing that note about The Thing?" Mr. Mayfair asked.

The boys nodded with embarrassment.

"And throwing out Anabelle's doll, and making footprints by the creek?"

"We didn't mean anything wrong—we just—" the boy hesitated.

"You just hated to lose your clubhouse," Mrs. Mayfair said, beginning to smile a little. "Well, I'm sure Roger and Anabelle won't mind if you come and play here with them sometimes."

"Sure," Roger said. "You can come here all you want."

He was glad no one knew about the note in his pocket.

The boys looked up at Roger cautiously. Anabelle stood quietly beside her mother. She was not sure what she thought of strange boys being in her tree house. She hoped they would not throw out her dolls anymore.

Twelve

That night Roger wrote a letter to Bobby Thompson.

DEAR BOBBY,

I like living in the country. There are two boys down the road, and I am going to join their club. Their names are Donald and Michael. The tree house is our clubhouse. They had the tree house for their clubhouse before we came out here, and they thought we wouldn't let them play in it anymore. So they tried to scare us away.

They used to secretly follow us through the woods sometimes. I heard them. And one time we found a piece of bread after they ate some sandwiches in the tree house.

They wrote a note to scare us and made big footprints on the ground so we would think there was a monster living around the tree house somewhere. They told me they made the footprints with a big piece of cardboard. They looked like this.

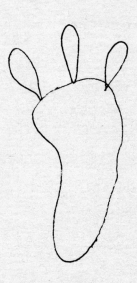

But they like me now, and they said I can join their club. They have a pony, and they said I can ride it sometimes. Donald collects baseball cards. He has a hundred. I am going to start a collection of pebbles. I have a big room, big enough for everything I want to collect. My room in town was too dinky.

When you come to visit, I will show you the creek and the tree house.

Your friend,
ROGER

About the Author

Carol Beach York was born in Chicago, Illinois, and attended schools in Chicago and in Harvey, Illinois, where she and her daughter, Diana, now make their home.

The Tree House Mystery is her seventeenth book and she has also contributed to such magazines as *Seventeen, Highlights for Children*, and *Grade Teacher*.

About the Artist

Reisie Lonette also illustrated *The Haunted Birdhouse* and *The Library*. In addition to her free-lance work, she is a book designer and illustrator in residence for a publishing house.

She was born in New York City and now lives in Stewart Manor, New York, with her daughter, Marisa, and her son, Mark.